Magic
Animal Friends

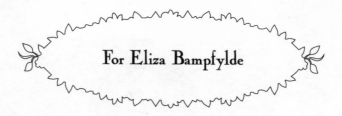

For Eliza Bampfylde

Special thanks to Conrad Mason

ORCHARD BOOKS

First published in Great Britain in 2018 by The Watts Publishing Group

1 3 5 7 9 10 8 6 4 2

Text copyright © Working Partners Ltd 2018
Illustrations copyright © Working Partners Ltd 2018
Series created by Working Partners Ltd

A CIP catalogue record for this book is available from the British Library.

ISBN 978 1 40834 709 6

Printed in Great Britain

MIX
Paper from
responsible sources
FSC® C104740

The paper and board used in this book are made from wood from responsible sources

Orchard Books
An imprint of Hachette Children's Group
Part of The Watts Publishing Group Limited
Carmelite House, 50 Victoria Embankment, London EC4Y 0DZ

An Hachette UK Company
www.hachette.co.uk
www.hachettechildrens.co.uk

Jasmine Whizzpaws' Rescue Race

Daisy Meadows

ORCHARD

Scribble Thicket

Stationery Station

Toadstool Cafe

r Cleverfeather's venting Shed

Woollyhop Shop

Forest Halt Station

Harmony Hall Theatre

easure Tree

Moo-Moo Milkshake Hut

Sparklepaw Cottage

Garland Green

Map of Friendship Forest

Can you keep a secret? I thought you could!

Then I'll tell you about an enchanted wood.

It lies through the door in the old oak tree,

Let's go there now - just follow me!

We'll find adventure that never ends,

And meet the Magic Animal Friends!

Love,
Goldie the Cat

Contents

CHAPTER ONE

Kites in the Garden

"Perfect weather for kites!" whooped Jess Forester, as she and her best friend, Lily Hart, rushed out into Lily's garden. At the other end of the lawn was the barn where Lily's parents ran the Helping Paw Wildlife Hospital. The girls loved taking care of the little animals there.

It was a beautiful autumn day and the sun shone warm and bright, but a strong breeze rustled the treetops and blew golden leaves across the grass. Some of the animals had been put in pens outside and a litter of badger cubs was having fun chasing some of the fallen leaves.

The girls exchanged a grin as they launched their kites into the air. Jess had a big red one with a green ribbon, and Lily's was blue with a yellow ribbon.

Jess's kite sank down on the grass, but the wind caught Lily's and lifted it up into the sky, twirling and dancing on the end

of its string. A tiny
ball of fur dashed
between Jess's
feet and pounced
for the trailing
ribbons. It was Jess's little
tabby kitten, Pixie.

"You'll never catch it, you
silly kitty!" laughed Jess.

"That won't stop
her trying though!"
added Lily. "She's
so cute!"

Lily's kite

swooped down low, and Pixie scampered

after it. She pounced again, and caught

the ribbon in both front paws. At once

the kite lifted, pulling Pixie

up so that her back paws

scrabbled in the air for a

moment. The little kitten

let go and dropped to the

ground, her fur fluffing up

in fright.

"Poor Pixie!" said Lily,

rushing over to stroke her. "You

don't want to be a flying cat, do you?"

"Hey, do you see that?" gasped Jess,

pointing at something she'd spotted.

The girls peered into the hedgerow that ran along the edge of the garden. There it was again – a flash of golden fur, glinting in the sunshine.

"It's Goldie!" cried Lily.

The golden cat came strolling out of the hedgerow, her tail waving and her whiskers quivering in the breeze. Pixie darted over and nuzzled up against Goldie, purring happily.

"Hello, Goldie," said Jess. "What are you doing here? Are we going back to Friendship Forest again?"

 13

"Ooh, I hope so!" said Lily. "Another adventure!"

Their cat friend had taken them to Friendship Forest many times before. It was a magical place where all the animals could talk, and lived in cute little houses.

Goldie let out a soft miaow. Then she raced across the grass, the wind flattening her fur. Quickly Lily and Jess reeled in their kites and tucked them under a garden chair for safekeeping. Then they told Pixie they'd be right back, and ran after Goldie. They knew that no time

passed in their world whilst they were in
Friendship Forest, so Pixie wouldn't have
to wait long.

The golden cat darted to the stream
at the bottom of the garden, and hopped
over the stepping stones into Brightley
Meadow. She raced up to a huge, dead
oak tree that stood alone in the middle of
the field. The Friendship Tree!

As Goldie approached, the tree burst
into life. Leaves sprouted from the twigs in

 15

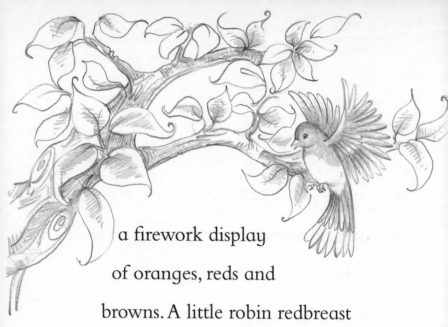

a firework display

of oranges, reds and

browns. A little robin redbreast

fluttered around the treetop, singing

merrily.

Goldie laid her paw against the trunk,

and at once words took shape in the bark,

as though written by an invisible hand.

Jess joined arms with Lily as they read

out loud together. "Friendship Forest!"

No sooner had they spoken than a

 16

little door formed in the tree trunk, with a handle shaped like a leaf. Lily stepped forward and twisted the handle. The door creaked open and golden light spilled from inside.

Together, the girls stepped through.

A warm tingle spread through their bodies, as though they were sunbathing on a summer's day, and they knew they were magically shrinking, just a little. For an instant all they could see was the golden light. Then it faded, and they found themselves standing in a familiar woodland glade.

The leaves above them were rustling furiously, and the branches of the trees were shaking in a fierce wind. The breeze buffeted the girls, gusting at their clothes and tangling their hair. Jess and Lily pulled their coats tight around themselves. Friendship Forest wasn't usually like this! Normally, it was a lovely place to be, whatever the weather.

"Thank goodness you're here!" cried a familiar voice over the howling of the wind.

Turning, the girls saw Goldie standing on her hind legs, her glittery scarf flying

like a flag. She was as tall as the girls'
shoulders now.

"It's good to see you, Goldie!" called
Jess. "But what's happening? The forest is
never this windy."

"Is Grizelda up to something?"
wondered Lily.

The girls looked at each other and
shuddered.
Grizelda was
the meanest
person they
had ever met!
She was a

horrible witch who kept trying to take over Friendship Forest for herself, and force the animals who lived there to leave. Lily and Jess had always managed to put a stop to her wicked plans, but Grizelda never gave up.

"I hope not!" said Goldie, shivering in the wind.

But just then a horrible cackle rang through the trees.

Jess and Lily both felt their hearts sink. They'd know that nasty laugh anywhere.

"Oh no," said Lily.

"Grizelda!" she and Jess said together.

CHAPTER TWO

A Sprite Surprise

Jess, Lily and Goldie ran through the
forest, following the sound of Grizelda's
laughter. The wind made their eyes water
as they came panting into a clearing, and
stumbled to a halt in front of the Treasure
Tree, which towered above them. It was
the tallest tree in the forest and the place

where the animals got most of their food.
It had fruits and nuts growing on every
branch, though some were tumbling down
in the wind.

"I think the laughter is coming from up
there," said Lily, peering into the branches.

"Look!" gasped Goldie, pointing.

On the highest branch perched a
woman with long, straggly green hair,
wearing a sparkly purple tunic and a
black cloak. She was cackling to herself.

"Grizelda!" said Jess. "What are you up
to now? I hope you've come to say sorry
for being mean all the time!"

The witch

stopped laughing

and glared at them.

"Oh, very funny!" she snarled.

"You're the ones who will be sorry! You

can kiss your furry friends goodbye,

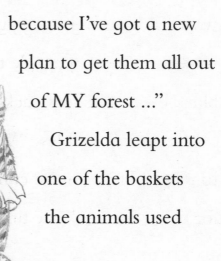

because I've got a new

plan to get them all out

of MY forest ..."

Grizelda leapt into

one of the baskets

the animals used

to collect their food. The basket came

whooshing down, gliding along a rope

on a pulley. As it reached the ground,

Grizelda stomped out of it.

"Take a look at this, girls," said the

witch, and she held out her hand. Sitting

in her palm was a tiny bottle with a

purple cork in it. Strange shapes swirled

inside it like smoke.

"What is it?" asked Goldie, suspiciously.

"Stupid cat!" cackled Grizelda. "It's a bottle, of course! It's what's inside it that's important. It's the wind sprites of Friendship Forest, all four of them – North, South, East and West! I caught them myself." She shook the bottle. "You in there – show yourselves!"

The swirling shapes pressed up against the inside of the bottle. Four little faces peered out, each one cute and round as a button, staring at the girls with big shiny eyes.

"Oh no," whispered Lily to Jess. "They

don't look very happy in there."

"The grey one is Gale," said Grizelda. "He's from the south wind. The green one is Gust; he lives on the east wind. The purple one is Huff, who lives on the west wind. And Puff is the blue one, the sprite of the north wind."

And with that she pulled out the cork.

There was a howling sound, so loud the girls and Goldie had to cover their ears. Then the grey

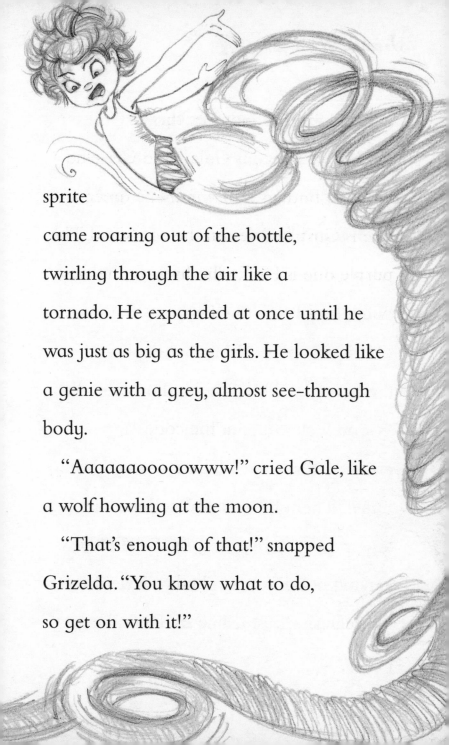

sprite

came roaring out of the bottle,

twirling through the air like a

tornado. He expanded at once until he

was just as big as the girls. He looked like

a genie with a grey, almost see-through

body.

"Aaaaaaooooowww!" cried Gale, like

a wolf howling at the moon.

"That's enough of that!" snapped

Grizelda. "You know what to do,

so get on with it!"

With another mournful howl, Gale twisted off through the air. Wherever he went, he barged into the trees, knocking them over like dominoes, and his whirling tail tore up bushes below as he disappeared into the forest.

Grizelda pushed the cork back into the bottle, cackling louder than ever. "Good luck stopping him, pests!" she crowed. "Soon the whole forest will be mine!" Then she clicked her fingers and disappeared with a flash and a BANG, leaving nothing behind but a little shower of green sparks smelling like rotten eggs.

"After him!" cried Jess. The girls raced off into the forest, with Goldie hot on their heels.

Gale was speeding so fast that he was soon out of sight, but it was easy to see where he had been. Behind him he had left a path of fallen trees and bushes

ripped from the ground. The girls followed
it, running as fast as they could.

"This is awful," wailed Goldie. "That
wind sprite is destroying the forest!"

"Don't worry, Goldie," called Lily.
"We'll stop him, won't we, Jess?"

"Of course we will!" said Jess, leaping
over a ripped-up
bumbleberry bush.
"Where do you
think he's
going?"

"I don't know,"
replied Goldie,

"but he's heading south."

Just then, something came speeding towards them in a little golden blur. The girls skidded to a halt, watching it nervously.

"Do you think it's another wind sprite?" asked Lily.

The golden blur leapt up on to a fallen tree trunk and stood there, panting, a pink tongue lolling out of its mouth.

"That's not a wind sprite!" laughed Jess. "It's a puppy!"

It was a cocker spaniel, covered head to tail in silky golden fur.

 31

"Hello," said Lily. "Wow, you're the
fastest puppy I've
ever seen!"

The puppy
wagged her tail
happily. "Oh,
thank you
so much! My
name is Jasmine
Whizzpaws and
I'm so glad
I've found you
because I really need your help!"

CHAPTER THREE

Earthquake!

Jasmine barely paused for breath. "You're Jess and Lily, aren't you? I've heard all about you and how kind and helpful you are, and my goodness, what a lot of trouble we're in, but now you're here it doesn't seem nearly so bad, and—"

"I'm sorry to interrupt," said Goldie

 33

gently. "But I'm afraid we're in a bit of a hurry!"

"We're trying to stop a wind sprite called Gale," said Jess.

Jasmine leapt to the ground. "Oh, I'm so sorry – I was gabbling again, wasn't

I? Mum says I do that all the time! But that's perfect, because I need to stop Gale too! I heard him say he's going to my home. He wants the

Master Map of Friendship Forest, you see."

"What's the Master Map?" asked Lily.

"It's a magical map which shows everything in Friendship Forest," said Jasmine. "Every time something new appears in the forest, it appears on the map straight away. And if something new appears on the map, it appears in the forest too!"

Lily and Jess exchanged an anxious glance.

"Uh-oh," said Jess. "This must be Grizelda's plan!"

"She doesn't just want to make the forest windy," said Lily. "She's trying to get her hands on the map too!"

"It's divided into four parts," Jasmine piped up. "My family look after the southern part. But anything Grizelda does to the south will soon spread to the rest of the forest!" The little puppy's ears drooped, and she sniffed sadly. "Can you imagine if she does destroy it all? Where would we all go?"

"That won't happen," said Jess firmly.

"We're going to help you," said Lily, giving Jasmine a stroke on her silky

head. "Gale won't get away with this, I
promise!"

"Oh thank you!" said Jasmine, perking
up at once and wagging her tail. "In that
case ... follow me!"

The girls ran on through the forest with
Goldie at their side, following the little
golden blur of Jasmine as she raced ahead.

"She really is the fastest puppy ever!" puffed Jess.

"Look!" cried Lily.

Jasmine had run into a big clearing, and right in the middle of it stood a tall, slender tower. Its walls were as smooth and white as the icing on a wedding cake, and at the very top of it, high above the treetops, was

a turret. The golden roof gleamed in the sunshine.

"This way!" called Jasmine. She opened a little golden door at the foot of the tower and darted inside.

The girls and Goldie followed Jasmine up a spiral staircase of white steps that wound round and round inside the tower. Every so often they passed a little window and caught a glimpse of the forest, farther and farther below. Soon they were out of breath, all except for Jasmine.

At last the puppy raced out into an enormous living room at the top of the

tower, where she skidded to a halt. "Oh no!" she yelped.

When Lily, Jess and Goldie caught up with her, they all gasped.

In the very middle of the room, Gale was fighting over something with two grown-up golden spaniels. Peering closer, the girls saw that it was a silver square of parchment the size of a large handkerchief.

"The southern part of the map!" cried Goldie.

The dogs each had hold of one corner of the parchment, and Gale had another.

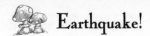

All three of them were tugging as hard as they could.

Jasmine darted across the room and snatched the fourth corner in her teeth.

The dogs staggered to and fro as they pulled against Gale, rumpling the soft red carpet they were standing on. They knocked over a cosy armchair, then a cupboard full of chew toys, scattering

them across the floor.

"That map's not yours!" Lily shouted at Gale. "Let go!"

But Gale just threw back his head and laughed. "Ha! Ha! Haaaaaaoooowww!" Then he began to twirl on the spot, spinning like a tornado.

Rrrrrriiip!

"The map!" yelled Goldie.

The silver parchment had torn in two, and the three spaniels went tumbling head over heels. Jasmine's mum and dad still clung on to one half, while Jasmine went rolling over and over until she stopped by Jess's feet.

Gale held up his half of the map in triumph. "Mine!" he howled.

Suddenly the tower seemed to shudder, and the girls and Goldie almost fell over.

"That felt like an earthquake!" said Goldie nervously.

The room shook again, and the friends clung on to each other. A rumbling sounded from below. Then – *CRACK!* – the floor split down the middle, as though

it were a biscuit snapped by a giant's fingers. The crack spread right across the room, tearing the ceiling and the walls apart. Jasmine's mum and dad were stranded, away from the staircase.

"Mum!" cried Jasmine. "Dad!"

Gale puffed out his cheeks and a fierce wind swept into the room, whipping the piece of map out of Mr and Mrs Whizzpaws' grip.

"Now I have both halves of the map and you have none!" Gale said with a horrid chuckle.

Then he blew the two pieces up

through the broken roof, sending them
fluttering away through the sky.

"Ha! Ha! Haaaaaaoooowww!"
laughed Gale again, then he shot up
through the roof, twirling after the two
halves of the map.

"Oh dear," called Mrs Whizzpaws
from the far side of
the tower. "The
ground has split
in two, just where
the map was torn.
And the split has gone
right through our

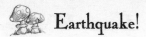

beautiful tower!"

"It's my fault," said Jasmine, hanging her head. "I wasn't fast enough."

"You're the fastest puppy we've ever known!" said Lily.

"Don't blame yourself, Jasmine," said Mr Whizzpaws. "We can fix this. The only problem is, we're stuck over here, and we can't reach the stairs!"

"We'll find the map!" said Jess and Lily together.

Jasmine smiled gratefully. "Oh, thank you both. I knew you'd help us!"

"We must find the two halves of the

map and put them back together," said Goldie.

"Let's go!" the friends cried, and they hurried out of the broken room. Lily and Jess hoped putting the map back together would be as easy as it sounded. If not, the animals would have nowhere to live!

CHAPTER FOUR

Flying Eclairs

Jasmine bounded down the stairs, two at a time. Lily, Jess and Goldie hurried after her, but the puppy was much too fast for them. As they reached the bottom of the tower, she was already disappearing into the forest.

"Wait for us, Jasmine!" cried Goldie.

Up above the treetops, the girls could still see two glittering scraps of parchment in the distance, flitting on the wind, before they disappeared. "If we keep going that way, we should catch her," said Lily.

"I think I can see something moving up ahead!" said Jess. "Come on!"

Together they ran into the forest, as fast as they could.

The friends were puffing and panting by the time they caught up with Jasmine. The little puppy had stopped in a clearing, next to the Nibblesqueak Bakery. It was a tiny pink cottage, even

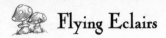

smaller than the girls, with a thatched
roof.

But something very strange was
happening there. The girls gasped in
astonishment as a jam roly-poly went
sailing out of an open window of the
bakery and hit a tree trunk. *SPLAT!*

"What's going on?" asked Goldie.

Two sparkleberry eclairs
shot out of the chimney
and slid down the roof,
leaving smears of cream. Then a
round hazelnut cake came rolling
out of the little front door.

"I don't understand!"
said Jasmine. "Who's
throwing— Ow!"
Something bounced
off her head and
fell on the ground.
"Someone's pelting
us with muffins!" said Goldie.

"It's not a muffin," said Lily, picking up the object that had hit Jasmine. A frayed old fluffy hamster toy sat in her hand. "It's Nutmeg, Olivia Nibblesqueak's favourite doll!"

Jess shook her head sadly. "Who's being so mean?"

Crouching low, the four friends darted to the window, dodging as a tray of blossom buns shot past them. When they were close enough to kneel down and peer inside, the girls spotted Olivia Nibblesqueak and her hamster family cowering behind the counter. In the

middle of the tiny bakery, a miniature
whirlwind raged, whistling and roaring
as it snatched up cakes and pastries and
flung them in every direction.

"It's not a person throwing cakes
at all!" said Jasmine. "It's a horrible
whirlwind!"

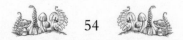

"I bet this is Gale's doing," muttered Goldie, but there was no sign of the wind sprite.

"Look!" said Lily.

Right in the middle of the swirling wind, a little scrap of silver parchment fluttered to and fro.

"It's one half of the map," said Jess.

"But how do we get it out of there?" Lily wondered.

"I don't know," said Goldie. "How do you stop a whirlwind?" Goldie frowned thoughtfully. "Oh yes! The Weather Watcher! She'll help us."

"The Weather what?" said Jess. Goldie had never mentioned her before.

"The Weather Watcher – Blossom Needlenose. She keeps an eye on the weather all over Friendship Forest," Goldie explained. "She's a hummingbird – Honey Needlenose's cousin!"

The girls grinned. They'd met Honey before, and they guessed that Blossom would be just as nice.

"If anyone knows how to stop this, it will be Blossom Needlenose," Goldie continued. "She lives in the Friendship Forest Weather Station."

"I know where that is!" said Jasmine. "I can go and get her. If I run at top speed, I'll be back here in no time."

As Jasmine raced off, Lily cautiously pushed the bakery door open wide. The roar of the whirlwind sounded even noisier now. "Nibblesqueaks!" she called above the din. "Over here!"

The hamsters stared at the girls from behind the counter, but their fur stood on end,

and they trembled with fear.

"I'm scared!" cried little Olivia
Nibblesqueak.

Lying on her belly, Jess reached through
the doorway. She reached in as far as
she could and Olivia jumped into her

hand. Jess pulled her out, past the raging
whirlwind, and placed her on the ground.

"Thank you!" Olivia said.

 58

Jess then went back and got the rest of
the family, one by one, scooping up each
animal and lifting them out. Lily shut the
door behind them, shutting the whirlwind
in the bakery.

"Phew!" gasped Mr Nibblesqueak, as
Jess put him down on the grass. "Thank
you, girls, what a relief!"

Lily handed Olivia her doll.

"Oh, thank you!" said Olivia. "That
naughty wind sprite has ruined our lovely
cakes and treats!"

"We'll fix it," Jess promised.

"Where is Gale now?" Lily asked.

 59

"We don't know. He came, blew through the door, made that horrible whirlwind and then whizzed off again," said Mrs Nibblesqueak, her voice still a little quivery.

"I just hope Jasmine comes back with Blossom soon," whispered Goldie, as the hamster family dusted each other off. "That whirlwind has to be stopped before it gets any bigger!"

CHAPTER FIVE

Jasmine to the Rescue

Luckily it wasn't long before the golden puppy came whizzing through the forest towards them.

"Jasmine!" cried Jess and Lily, as their friend skidded to a halt beside the bakery.

"And look," said Goldie, pointing out another little creature that had come

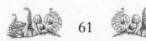

darting through the air behind Jasmine.
"There's Blossom Needlenose!"

"The Weather Watcher!" the girls cried
together.

Peering closer, the girls saw that it was
a bright blue and pink hummingbird,
with a slender beak and tiny wings
beating so fast they could hardly be seen.

"She looks so like Honey!" said Lily.

"I'll take that as a compliment," smiled
the hummingbird as she arrived. "Dear
Honey has told me so much about you!"
Blossom perched on the grass and took
off a little backpack. "Now, I've come to

see this whirlwind for myself."

As she rummaged inside her bag with
her beak, Jess caught a glimpse of all
kinds of strange instruments
inside. There was
a rainbow-
coloured
windsock,
a golden
weather vane

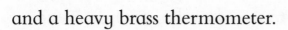

and a heavy brass thermometer.

Blossom dug out a funny object that
looked like a glittery pair of binoculars.
Then she flew up, still hovering as she

held the binoculars with her feet and used
them to spy through the window of the
bakery.

"Dear me!"
she exclaimed.
"That little
whirlwind is
the fastest I've
ever seen ... and
magical too, if I'm not mistaken. What
we need to stop a magical whirlwind is
something that can go very fast indeed,
but in the opposite direction from the way
the whirlwind is spinning." She frowned

thoughtfully. "But what in all the forest could be fast enough?"

"What about Jasmine?" said Jess. "She's fast!"

Blossom nodded thoughtfully. "That's not a bad idea!"

"But do you really think I can do it?" said Jasmine nervously.

"We know you can!" said both girls together.

The little puppy wagged her tail proudly. "All right, then," she said. "I'll give it a try!"

Goldie swung open the door of the

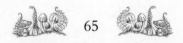

bakery, and Jasmine ducked inside.

"Go, Jasmine!" shouted Lily, peering through the window. Then she had to dodge as a gooseberry doughnut went *SPLAT* against the window frame.

Jasmine leapt straight into the whirlwind. Her eyes closed and her fur streamed back as she fought against it. At first she struggled so much it looked as though she was running in slow motion. Then she began to speed up, racing in a circle round the edge of the whirlwind.

"I think it's working!" called Jess, squeezing in next to Lily. "Keep going!"

Jasmine kept running, faster and faster, round and round the bakery. Gradually the roar of the wind died away until it was no more than a rustling breeze, then a whisper, then nothing at all. The map piece fell fluttering down on to the floor.

Jasmine snatched it up and tottered out of the bakery, panting with exhaustion.

The girls, Goldie and Blossom crowded

 67

round the little puppy, along with the Nibblesqueaks, patting Jasmine's back and ruffling her fur.

"Thank you so much!" said the Nibblesqueaks. "You saved our bakery!"

Goldie hugged Jasmine. "And you saved the map too!"

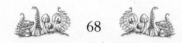

"I feel dizzy!" said Jasmine.

"Aaaaaaaaaoowww!"

The howl came from just behind them and they jumped. The girls turned to see Gale's round grey face glaring out from among the trees. The wind sprite's big eyes bulged with fury. "You naughty girls!" he wailed. "Ruining all my fun! Well, you'll never get the second piece of the map ... I'll make sure of it! Aaaaoooowww!"

Then he whipped away, whirling off through the forest.

"What do you think he's going to do?"

said Jasmine nervously.

"Whatever it is, we'd better stop him,"
said Lily. "And fast!"

Jess took the piece of map and tucked
it into her pocket. The girls rushed after

the wind sprite, with
Jasmine and Goldie hot
on their heels.

"He went that way!"
said Goldie, pointing
to a trail of smashed-
up trees that wound
through the forest.

As they ran, they

passed fallen beech trees and spotted toadstools. All through the forest, little animals were scurrying to get home and close their doors and windows to stay safe from the wind.

It wasn't long before the friends came stumbling out of the trees into an open glade.

"Oh, no!" gasped Jess.

Just in front of them, the ground fell away in a steep cliff face. A jagged chasm ran right through the middle of the forest. There was no way across, and the gap was much too wide to jump over. A fierce

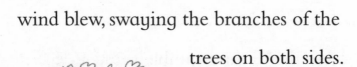

wind blew, swaying the branches of the

trees on both sides.

"I've never seen

anything like this

before!" said Goldie.

"It must be the

rip in the map,"

said Lily.

She

peered

over the

edge, but the

chasm was so deep

that she couldn't see

the bottom of it.

Then the ground rumbled, and some clumps of soil and grass fell from the edge of the cliff, tumbling into the darkness far below.

"It's getting even wider!"

said Jasmine. Her ears drooped in despair. "Oh dear ... we can't follow Gale and get the second half of the map!"

Unless the friends could put the magical map back together, the forest would be torn in two for ever.

CHAPTER SIX

Kite Trees

"There must be some way to get to the other side," said Jess with determination. "We just have to find it!"

They started to walk along the side of the chasm.

"Hey, I've never seen leaves like that," said Lily, pointing at a fallen tree. The leaves on it were huge, dark green and shaped like diamonds.

"It's called the kite tree," said Goldie.

"That's it!" Lily snapped her fingers. "They look just like the kites we were flying back home, but bigger!"

"Of course!" said Jess. "I bet we can use them to lift us up and over the chasm."

Quickly the friends each picked a leaf and held the stalk tight. Then they stood side by side at the edge of the cliff. The wind was still blowing, buffeting the leaves and almost tearing them from the girls' hands.

"All together now," said Goldie. "Three, two, one … *Jump!*"

The four friends leaped up high over the chasm, clinging on tight to their leaves. Lily and Jess held their breath. Any moment now, they might go plummeting down ...

But at once the wind caught the kites, blowing them up high. It took all their strength to hold on as they bobbed in the air, like puppets dangling on strings.

"Wheeeee!" cried Goldie, twirling past.

"We're flying!" gasped Jasmine.

The wind blew them all across, and

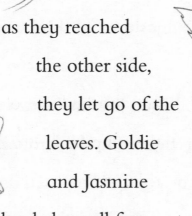

as they reached
the other side,
they let go of the
leaves. Goldie
and Jasmine
landed on all four
paws, and the girls dropped
down next to them.

"Wow!" said Lily, as she pushed
back her wind-tousled hair.

"That was amazing," said Jess, as the
four kites flew away.

"It certainly was," said Goldie. "But
now we need to catch Gale ..."

"Look!" cried Jasmine. "I think I see him!"

The girls followed Jasmine's gaze and spotted a grey figure flitting through the forest not far away. Quickly they dashed through the trees, and saw that Gale was twirling on the spot next to a pretty little cottage. Beyond, a lovely green meadow stretched out, full of flowers in every colour of the rainbow.

"That's Garland Green," said Lily.

"And Sparklepaw Cottage," said Jess. The Sparklepaw family of cats were friends of theirs.

"But what's Gale doing?" Jasmine cried.

The wind was growing stronger and stronger, gusting through the meadow and ripping up petals which danced on the breeze. Then Gale drew in a deep breath, puffed and a whirlwind sprang up out of the ground.

The girls gasped as the whirlwind grew bigger. It was much larger than the

one that had wrecked the Nibblesqueak
bakery. But it kept on growing, until it
was twice the height of the wind sprite,
then taller still. It ripped at the bushes
and sent a tree toppling over. Then with a
flick of Gale's wrist, the massive whirlwind
surged towards the cottage …

"Oh no!" gasped Lily. "We have to help
the Sparklepaws!"

CHAPTER SEVEN

A Whirlwind of Trouble

"Ha ha haaaaaooooww!" howled Gale. "My whirlwind will tear that house apart, and the map too!"

"The map must be in the whirlwind, like last time!" said Goldie.

Sure enough, the girls could see a little

scrap of silver flashing in the centre of the
swirling wind.

Amelia Sparklepaw, a fluffy white
cat, appeared at the window of the
cottage. Then the rest of her family – Mrs
Sparklepaw, Timmy and Tommy, all just
as white and fluffy as she was, gathered
around her. Their fur stood on end with

fright, and Amelia's big blue eyes glittered with tears. "What's happening?" she cried through the window.

"Don't worry!" Jess shouted, over the roar of the whirlwind. "We'll put a stop to it!"

"Do you think you can stop this whirlwind, like you did at the bakery?" Lily asked Jasmine.

The little golden puppy looked nervous, but she nodded bravely. "It's much, much bigger ... but I'll do my best!"

Jasmine set off once again, darting into the whirlwind and running round the

outside of it. She ran slowly at first, then faster and faster.

"I've never seen anything so speedy in my life!" said Jess.

But Gale drew in a deep breath and blew, puffing out his cheeks with a great rushing sound.

At once, the whirlwind swelled to twice the size, like an inflating balloon. Now it was so loud that the girls had to cover their ears. Jasmine was

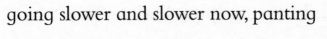

going slower and slower now, panting
with the effort, her little
pink tongue hanging
out.

The
Sparklepaws'
cottage
shuddered and
began to rise up,
carried by the
force of the winds.
Jasmine fell head
over heels, tossed across

Garland Green as the whirlwind snatched up everything in its path.

"This is the most powerful whirlwind I've ever seen!" yelled Jess.

"Oh no, look at the Sparklepaws!" cried Lily.

The little white cats were trying to make a dash for it out of the cottage door, but they were too late and got swept up by the wind, tumbling like

clothes in a washing machine.

Gale laughed madly as the whirlwind
carried them all up, higher and higher
into the sky ...

"The whirlwind is too strong for me!"
yelped Jasmine, as she scrambled upright.
"I can't stop it!"

"Keep going!" shouted Goldie, her
whiskers plastered to her face by the
whirling winds. "If you can't do it, no one
can!"

Lily and Jess looked at each other.

"Did you hear what I heard?" said Lily.

"I think so," said Jess. "No one can do it.

89

But if we work as a team ..."

"It's worth a try!" said Lily. "Come on, Goldie!"

Lily, Jess and Goldie darted across Garland Green to Jasmine. They stood in a circle and then stepped right into the wind. It battered them, making their hair and fur stream back in the current.

"Three ... two ... one ..." counted Lily.

"GO!" shouted both girls.

The four friends began to run. At first it felt like wading through treacle. It was all Lily and Jess could do to put one foot in front of the other. But as they

glanced to the side, they saw their friends
running with them, eyes gleaming with
determination. And gradually, it became
easier and easier. Faster they went, faster
and faster ...

And at last, the roar of the wind began
to calm.

"It's working!" whooped Jasmine. "We're slowing the whirlwind!"

Gradually, the cottage began to sink downwards, like a kite drifting on a gentle breeze. *Thump!* It landed softly, as the last of the wind died away.

The four friends collapsed on the ground, panting and laughing with the effort. All around them, Lily and Jess saw the Sparklepaws come floating down on to the grass, their white fur all fluffed up by the wind.

The girls hugged. "We did it!"

CHAPTER EIGHT

Good Riddance!

"Look!" cried Goldie. "It's the map!"

The girls spotted the second little silver scrap of parchment come fluttering down like confetti from the sky.

"Noooooooo!" howled Gale. But before he could snatch the map, Jasmine leapt up and caught it in her mouth.

"Give up, Gale," said Jess. "The map belongs with Jasmine's family, and that's where it'll stay!"

"You pests!" spluttered Gale. "You nuisances!" But there was nothing he could do.

Lily had one piece of the map, and

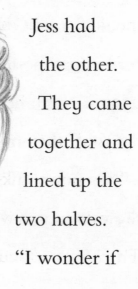

Jess had the other. They came together and lined up the two halves. "I wonder if

…" Jess started, but she didn't have to wonder for long, because soon the whole map was covered with a magical silvery glow. A flash of light, almost like thunder, zipped down the tear. Lily and Jess closed their eyes at the brightness. When they opened them a second later the map had mended itself! The two halves were fixed back together and the map was whole again.

"Yay!" they both cried.

"Do you think—" started Jasmine, but she was cut off when the ground shook. There was a loud rumbling sound.

"The chasm is closing up!" called
Goldie. The girls turned and watched as
the two parts of the forest came together
again. Even the trees that had fallen over
creaked upright, so that all the damage
Gale had done vanished completely.

"And look at the
tower!" said Jess,
pointing to the
Whizzpaws' home.

In the distance, the two halves of the broken white tower came together until it stood straight and tall, in one piece again.

At last the rumbling came to an end, and the forest stood just as calm and peaceful as it usually was.

Craa-aack!

Green and yellow sparks flew among the flowers of Garland Green and Grizelda appeared. She was scowling furiously. "Bristling broomsticks!" she snapped. "That map was part of my plan, and you meddlers have wrecked it!"

"Good!" said Lily.

"You should be ashamed of yourself, picking on animals," said Jess.

Grizelda just sniffed and glowered at Gale. "And you, so-called wind sprite, what do you have to say for yourself? You're useless! Back in the bottle with you!"

She whipped the little bottle out from under her cloak and pulled out the purple stopper. Gale let out a long, mournful howl as he was sucked back into the bottle, like a cobweb into a vacuum cleaner. "Aaaaaaooooow!"

Grizelda bunged the stopper back in,

 98

leaving Gale blinking out sadly at them all, trapped with the three other wind sprites. "This isn't over, girls," snarled the witch. "Mark my words ... I'll drive all the animals out, then Friendship Forest will be mine for ever!"

The witch cackled madly. Then there was another *craa-aaack!* And with a shower of smelly green sparks, she was gone.

"Good riddance!" said Goldie.

Jasmine Whizzpaws snuggled up to the girls, wagging her tail happily. "Thank you so much!" she said. "Because of you, our map is back to normal!"

"We did it together, remember?" said Lily.

"And we never could have done it without your amazingly fast running!" added Jess. "Just promise us one thing. If that wicked witch comes back, you'll call us straight away."

"You can count on it!" said Jasmine.

The girls gave her the silver map. Then

the little puppy dashed away, now just
a golden blur racing towards the white
tower that was her home.

"Looks like our adventure is over," said
Lily sadly.

"For now," said Goldie with a smile. "I'll
take you home. But you'll be back soon.'

The girls nodded – of course! – and
Goldie led them back to the Friendship
Tree.

In no time at all, the girls found
themselves standing in Brightley Meadow
again. The sun was still shining, and the
wind blew, rustling the grass and making

the leaves dance. Laughing, the girls ran across the stepping stones back into the garden, where they took up their kites and launched them into the sky.

As the colourful diamonds of fabric swooped and dived through the air, little Pixie the kitten raced in circles on the grass, trying to catch the trailing ribbons.

"I can't believe how fast she's going!" said Lily.

"In fact, I can only think of one little animal that goes faster ..." said Jess.

The girls grinned at each other, both thinking of their new friend Jasmine

Whizzpaws and of all the other incredible animals that were now safe and happy in Friendship Forest.

The End

Best friends Lily and Jess are excited to be going to a musical show in Friendship Forest! But when they get there, the wicked witch Grizelda puts a curse on the place, knocking everything out of sync. Can adorable fawn Daisy Tappytoes help Friendship Forest regain its rhythm?

Find out in the next Magic Animal Friends book,

Daisy Tappytoes Dares to Dance

Turn over for a sneak peek ...

Jess Forester woke suddenly. For a moment, she wondered where she was. Then she remembered. She was having a sleepover at her best friend Lily Hart's house! But what had woken her?

Tap tap tap tap!

Jess poked the bundle of covers in the next bed. "Wake up!"

Lily's sleepy face appeared. She opened one eye.

"Listen," said Jess.

Tap tap tap tap!

"I think it's coming from outside," Jess said. "But what could it be?"

Lily sat up.

"I think I know! It must be the woodpecker Mum and Dad have been looking after. They said he was feeling better." She jumped out of bed. "Let's get dressed and go and see him!"

Tap tap tap tap tap!

Jess laughed. "He definitely sounds better!"

Minutes later, the girls ran down the garden towards Helping Paw Wildlife Hospital. It was run by Mr and Mrs Hart inside their barn. Lily and Jess loved all animals, and adored helping to look after the patients.

Nearby was the aviary – a huge tent made of netting, big enough for birds to fly around in. Jess spotted a jackdaw with a bandaged leg, a tiny sparrow and a robin with missing tail feathers.

Tap tap tap tap tap!

"There's the woodpecker." Lily pointed to a green bird with bandaged wings. Its red-topped head bobbed back and forth as it knocked at a tree stump with its long, strong beak.

Jess crouched down close to the netting. "You'll soon be flying again, little one," she said softly.

"Let's see how the rabbits are doing," suggested Lily.

They found two baby bunnies outside their hutch, sniffing the morning air with their snuffly noses. Jess was leaning into the run to stroke them, when her eye was caught by a flash of gold beside the hay store.

Read

Daisy Tappytoes Dares to Dance

to find out what happens next!

Magic
Animal Friends

Can Jess and Lily save the magic of
Friendship Forest from Grizelda?
Read all of series eight to find out!

COMING SOON!
Look out for
Jess and Lily's
next adventure:
Bertie Bigroar Finds His Voice!

3 stories
in 1!

www.magicanimalfriends.com

If you like
Magic Animal Friends,
you'll love…

Welcome to Animal Ark!

Animal-mad Amelia is sad
about moving house, until she discovers
Animal Ark, where vets look after all
kinds of animals in need.

*Join Amelia and her friend Sam for a
brand-new series of animal adventures!*

Can you keep the secret?

There's lots of fun for everyone at
www.magicanimalfriends.com

Play games and explore the secret world of
Friendship Forest, where animals can talk!

Join the
Magic Animal Friends Club!

✦ Special competitions ✦
✦ Exclusive content ✦
✦ All the latest Magic Animal Friends news! ✦

To join the Club, simply go to

www.magicanimalfriends.com/join-our-club/